Leo and David
A TALE OF TWO ANGELS

by

Luca Leonvago

RoseDog🐾Books
PITTSBURGH, PENNSYLVANIA 15238

RoseDog Books
585 Alpha Drive
Pittsburgh, PA 15238
Visit our website at www.rosedogbookstore.com

ISBN: 978-1-4809-7879-9
eISBN: 978-1-4809-7902-4

To my Dave, my brother Fulvio, Mamma, Papa, Grandaunt Giovanna, and Grand-mama Rosa.

Leo and David

One day at an arts university, a professor in his 50s was just coming out from his office to go back home when a student holding an old magazine borrowed from the library ran up to him and with panting breath, asked, "Professor, is this true? Is this you, professor?"

The professor leaned in to look more closely at the cover of the magazine. For a moment, he stalled and then opened the pages. There were pictures, a lot of pictures, inside. So many it was overwhelming.

"Do you really want to know who this man is on the cover?" asked the professor.

The student, who was ready to listen and curious about the whole story replied immediately, "Yes!"

. . .

Once upon a time, in a kingdom surrounded by water and far away, there was a royal family which had been on the throne for more than 1000 years. This was my country, my kingdom, and they were my family. When I was living there, my grandmother reigned. She was an exceptional woman—strong, intelligent, and capable of resolving any political or familial problem with extraordinary foresight. My Mum, the Crown Princess, was next in line. We were a large family, with five brothers and two sisters, as well as uncles, aunts, and numerous cousins from both maternal and paternal sides.

When I was a small child, my nurse, who I used to call *Lady of the Garden* because she had a very difficult name to pronounce, would read me all sorts of stories and fairy tales. My favorite was *The Happy Prince*. I never forgot some of the lines:

> *"In a bed in the corner of the room, her little boy is lying ill. He has a fever, and is asking for oranges. His mother has nothing to give him but river water, so he is crying. Swallow, Swallow, little Swallow, will you not bring her the ruby out of my sword-hilt?"*

The relationship between the swallow and the happy prince touched my heart and stayed with me. When I turned eighteen, I felt that my duty was to relieve all the misery in my country, like the little swallow and the happy prince. So I started to go out in disguise late in the evening to help people that, thanks to my nurse, I knew were experiencing difficulties and needed help. These late-night escapades were soon noticed and, without me knowing or suspecting, I was followed. The guards reported to my Mother, who by then had become queen, but they lied and completely distorted my actions. They made her believe that I was spending my time drinking, dancing, and associating with bad people.

One night, in one of the larger rooms where we used to sit after dinner and spend some quality family time together, I was vehemently attacked by my brothers. They accused me in front of my mother of going to bad places and spending a fortune on alcohol. I tried to defend myself, but my mother did not believe me. After all, I couldn't blame her. It was their word against mine. I was alone. They started to say I was crazy, that I wasn't fit to reign. They told her she had to make a drastic decision. What decision? What had they in mind?

Furious at the betrayal, I decided to go and see for myself what place I was supposedly going to. And I decided to go with a guard who had always been very protective of me.

Many people were out of the inn, drinking and talking loudly with their glasses in their hands. I had disguised myself as best I could and thought that no one would recognize me. But I was wrong. As if a light went out suddenly from a dark mass, just lit by only two street lamps that were on either side of the inn, I saw two ice brown eyes staring at me with a sly smile. I should have known what that smile meant: I know who you are! Someone recognized me.

My guard and I hesitated before going in further to the crowd, waiting on the other side of the sidewalk. Alfredo, this was his name I discovered later, came towards us, very determinedly introduced himself to us, and started to converse and invited us to have a drink inside. Both my guard and I didn't see anything wrong, and we spent all night chatting, drinking and laughing till very late. I started to go out with this person and in my naivety; I thought I had found my sparrow. I, who at that time, was no longer a happy prince.

We used to go out a lot, especially in the evenings, and he used to tell me things like, "I cannot spend a day without seeing you. Let's see each other even for five minutes." And I believed his affection towards me was sincere.

"La stolta gioventu' porgea l'orecchio mentre tutto attorno il mondo declina e peggiorando invecchia" wrote once Metastasio in Adrian in Syria.

At that time, I was very busy with my university studies to finish and state and family duties, and I was also engaged to a princess named Claudia who was very fond of me. Sadly, I didn't recognize her fondness as sincere. I felt her unconditional love when it was too late.

But let's go back to Alfredo. Where was I? Oh, yes. I remember now. After months of intense courtship, he asked to be closer to me, and he moved to my apartment. A few months later, I realized what a huge mistake I had made and precisely who I had next to me.

He once told that his ex-wife was crazy and that was why he had to divorce her. When I asked why she was crazy, he replied, "She was throwing me plates almost every night when I returned home." And then he added, "Because I was telling her I was going out for a walk after dinner, and instead I was going out having fun till 3:00 A.M. and she was waiting for me."

He laughed very loudly as he took a certain pride in what he was doing.

He always had a double life before and after me. For example, during his courtship, he used to ask me to come downstairs to see him, even if it was for five minutes. He wanted to keep me believing he was sincere. But he was running into some clubs or pubs till late in the morning to drink and have fun with other boys. I didn't realize that five minutes was a specific calculation. Other times, he assured me he had to go to see his sick mother or to go play bridge, but instead he was with other lovers.

A few times I saw him with my own eyes, frolicking on the rocky beach near our palace with strangers. God only knows what he was doing there. I tried to distance myself from him because I realized I neglected almost everything and everyone, including Claudia. She had the patience of a saint and forgave me. She didn't know the nature of our friendship.

Meanwhile, my relationship with my family had fallen apart. I had to leave. Alfredo was insisting to go out of the palace so he could manipulate me more easily. And so I did.

We rented a place near the sea, and we started to live together. The abuses went out of control. He was violent and abusive, not only physically but mentally. He kept telling me that everyone else was more beautiful and smarter than me, that no one wanted me as friend and I had only him. He said that my kindness made me stupid. He managed to alienate everyone until I was all alone with him.

4

Worst, he was humiliating me in public. He tried in every possible way to make me forget that I was young with a good heart. Once, at a costume ball, a man asked him rudely, "Where did you find him?" And his reply was, "In the rubbish bin." He was indeed, although 14 years older, considered still a handsome man. He was always tanned, and his body looked a lot like the Neptune sculpture in the city of Bologna. He never worked as he was living at his father's expense, so he always had all the free time you could possibly imagine for parties and lovers.

My family soon replaced me with my brother George for daily tasks and duties because I didn't appear reliable anymore. This would soon turn into a full replacement of my role. But before being fully and officially deposed, I was still taking care of some duties, ones very dear to me, despite Alfredo's pressure to give up completely.

At that time, there was a still-young empress who was exiled to our kingdom with her children and grandchildren. Her husband was murdered by rioters during a revolution that tore apart her country forever. He had no time to escape. One spring day, he was alone in his palace along with the Queen Mother and his sister with her son. The rest of the family had already moved to their summer residence. A group of colonels had organized a coup. They arrived at the palace gates with tanks, took all the members of the royal family who remained in the city prisoner, and carried them out into the hall and began firing machine guns. They didn't even spare the elderly Queen Mother or the son of the king's sister, who was only 17 years old at the time. We read with horror that the bodies were torn to pieces and sold on the street as souvenirs.

The only fault of this poor and unfortunate emperor had been to love his people too much. He had been determined to modernize and to develop his country. During his reign, the country had ranked number one in that part of the world for progress and development. He was so proud each time he opened a new school, a new hospital or a new road.

Another of his missions had been the emancipation of women and to recognize equality between women and men. Unfortunately, some of his very corrupt political rivals were against these reforms, and for greed, money, and power organized the coup.

While this happened, the empress and her children were in her summer residence—a beautiful, all-white villa with gardens that sloped down to the sea. A telegram warned her of the incident and, in a state of absolute shock, she managed to get on a ship with the children, insisting to carry with her all the paintings of her husband that were in the palace, knowing too well that they would be destroyed. The lady in waiting that had to pass the telegram understood the terrible situation and helped the empress to prepare for their departure.

The empress ran in the garden and began to call out loud the names of her children. When they finally were all together at the front door of the villa she said to them, "My children, now go into your room and take what is personal and dear to you, put it in a suitcase, and meet me in half an hour in my studio. Unfortunately, we have to leave our country. I will explain everything later."

The empress with her children, two boys and three girls, and the staff in service at the villa boarded a ship that would take them to my kingdom.

My mother loved the empress very much, and I went to visit her often. We always went to the opera together, and my mother used to play the national anthem of the empress's country in her honor. Everyone stood and listened to it out of respect.

The empress and I started a beautiful and affectionate friendship, and I had tea with her at least once a week. Once I recall I had to go on an official visit to her country for diplomatic reasons. So few days before my departure, I went to visit as usual, and so we talked.

The room in which we took our tea was bright and airy and conducive for talking. "Your Majesty," I began, "have you read the news that I must to go?"

The empress replied promptly, "I read it, my dear."

Taking my tea, I continued, "They informed us that we will stay at your home."

"My home?" the empress replied with an incredulous tone.

"Forgive me, Your Majesty. For me it will be always your home. I was wondering if there is anything I can bring you," I said, almost embarrassed but glad to be able to return something she was particularly fond of.

The empress paused a little before continuing

"My dear friend, of the material things I left at home that day…No, I don't want anything. I want things to stay there as they were when we left, and I pray to God that my children will one day return to their home and recognize places so dear to us all. But there is one thing you can do for me," continued the empress. "In all these years of exile, many times journalists have asked me about my jewelry. Believe me, I never thought about these things. For me it was only a uniform I wore as a soldier wears his to serve and represent my country, but there are two things I would like to get back. In my bedroom, in my closet on the left, there should be a box with tapes with the voices of my children when they were little when they started to talk. That box, yes, I would like that back. How nice would it be to listen to those tapes with their voices playing with their father? There is also another thing. In my nightstand, in the top drawer along with a bible which I hope is still there, inside there should be a drawing made by a little girl for me. She gave it to me on my coronation day. The king had wanted to organize a grand ceremony as a symbol of the emancipation of women. Crowning me as the first empress of the country, he wanted to crown all the women to tell them with this symbolic gesture, 'You are free to decide your future; you are free to aspire to whatever you want to be and do; you have equal rights and opportunities. You are the architect of your destiny.'"

On my coronation day, while my husband and I were passing by the main avenue of our capital on a carriage, this little girl, evading the guards, and with an impetus of joy, reached us, and she said, "Daddy King, I made this gift for you. We love you so much!" and she gave us this picture. She'd started going to one of the schools my husband opened. She had drawn the two of us and added a few words: "Thank you king. I feel free today. I am happy to be a girl today."

The guards, fearing some kind of attack, ran towards us, but my husband immediately reassured them and explained it was just a simple gift of love. The carriage stopped, and the little girl got in. At that precise moment, an ovation warmed our hearts, and we decided to have her with us for the entire ceremony. People were moved by the little girl's spontaneity. In the carriage, the little girl told us to put the drawing in our nightstand and added that each time we were sad we were supposed to look at it and be happy because she loved us so much.

My husband gave her his ring and told her, "When you go back home, give this to your mum and tell her that the king wants you to go to the university."

She hugged him. The girl's mother had meanwhile approached the carriage, calling the little girl to come back towards her.

Then, following my husband's words, I said, "Take also this ring. Put it in your pocket. Don't show it to anyone until you are at home. Give to your mom, and tell her it must be used for your studies."

"Okay," said the little girl.

"We said goodbye, and she returned to her mother, who was waiting next to a guard. You see, that drawing, yes, I would like to have it again next to me. The mother wrote me a letter thanking me for the gift, and she reassured me that she would send her daughter to university. And she kept her promise. That child became first a lawyer and then a judge. I was so proud of her. She even came to see me before we left our country, and that was the last time I saw her. I learned after the revolution that she couldn't practice under the new regime. But she continued to defend the rights of women and children secretly offering advice and assistance."

I left Her Majesty and went back to the palace to prepare for my departure.

The arrival was formal but cold. They brought me into the former royal palace, and after showing us our rooms, they left us alone to rest before the state dinner. I was very tired but decided to take a tour through the rooms and asked a guard why there were these barricades that made it look like a museum. The answer chilled me.

The guard said, "This is a museum! Almost all the royal palaces are museums. Who knows, yours might be too, one day."

For a moment, I froze, imagining tourists looking through our personal items. I smiled and changed the subject. An old lady came to rescue me and gently told me to follow her.

When we were alone, I said, "Madame, I am not hiding that your former empress is very dear to me. What happened to the personal belongings of the royal family? I promised to recover and return two objects that have only a great emotional value to her."

"I know where things are," she replied. "And I want to help you. You see, I was here before the revolution. A few months after the revolution, everything strictly personal was put in boxes and hidden in the garage along with coaches and cars used by the family. I have a copy of the key and private access to the garage. It is too risky for you to go personally, so I will go and bring you back what you are looking for.

"I will bring it into your room and hide them in your luggage. You must continue your official visit without arousing any suspicion. I know where everything is, and it will be easier for me to find them. After all, I was the only one that put away everything to avoid any theft of the items. I dare not to imagine the excitement that she will feel opening these boxes. They contain so many, many memories, equally both happy and sad. The dictatorship is trying very hard to cover all positive things achieved during their time. What it was almost comic is that while I was there, I read a newspaper article accusing the former king of having destroyed his own palace simply because he wants to add three new rooms for his children. What nonsense."

The day of my departure came, and I was full of many conflicting emotions. On the one hand, I was happy because I was returning home, but on the other hand, I was sad because I wanted to take the old lady with me. I was also very angry at the same time for the cold and contemptuous reception of this new military regime and the backwardness they seemed to inflict on the people.

When I arrived home, I rushed to see the empress, I couldn't wait any longer, I wanted to give her the tapes with the voices of her children and the little girl's drawing. But I had another surprise for her. The woman who had been so good to me and helped me to find the objects among all the boxes stored in the garage was with me, too. I had managed in secret to get her in the ship that had brought me back home. The two women hugged each other and cried. The lady gave to the empress a bag of soil from her motherland. I looked at the empress, nodded farewell, and left.

During my absence, the people who wanted me out had continued to work on their efforts to slander me. In the few weeks I was away, they managed to make me, in the eyes of my mother, an absolute dissolute, devoted to parties and alcohol, and someone who was slowly squandering his patrimony.

I was suddenly called for a family meeting with the Prime Minister and several representatives of the parliament. I arrived completely unprepared. It was decided that I would abdicate in favor of my brother, officially for "health reasons."

This had another effect. I would have to break off my engagement with Princess Claudia and live in exile, only to return to my country with the permission of the parliament. In return, I would receive a salary that would allow me to live abroad. In despair, I went to Alfredo, and in tears I told him what had just happened. I had only 48 hours to give an answer.

He understood at once that there was a chance to turn my misfortune into a lucrative opportunity. He said, "Perfect! This way we will be always be together without any problems. Accept immediately, and let's start to move as soon as possible."

I decided, "We will go to live in Paris, and I know precisely in which hotel."

And so, it was decided for me. I left Alfredo, and I went on horse to see Princess Claudia, who already knew the outcome of the meeting and was waiting for me on the porch of her family home. There was no need to say much as we always understood each other just simply by looking in the eyes of one another. Tears began to fall on our cheeks, and so I said goodbye to her one last time.

The day of my departure, there was no one to see me leave. The only people there were the guards to escort me. Later I found out that it was on that day the prime minister announced my "decision." This sudden announcement and my immediate departure, along with a ministerial ban on any public witnessing the event, meant that not one public soul saw me off. But despite this, my Aunt Giovanna challenged the minister's order and came to greet me. When she arrived, the guards that knew about the order didn't dare say anything or even try to stop her.

She came close to the carriage, and she gave me a small box with a "G" embroidered on the lid and said, "Goodbye, my dear Leo. I am old and I don't know if I will see you again, but please take this box and open it only if you are in serious troubles when you arrive at your destination. Put it in the hotel safe. Don't leave it in your room. And forget about it. Remember it must only be opened if you are in need. And now go. Your Aunt Giovanna must return home before they notice that I am not there."

The well-orchestrated plan of my frail health, the way they had painted me as both mentally and physically unstable and unable to rule, had in the end worked. I was seen as not capable of my duties and without the capacity to lead well. It worked, and I said goodbye to my country forever.

Alfredo and I arrived in Paris, and almost immediately, I realized in what jail I had ended up in and who my prison guard was. Ignoring any budget restrictions, we now had to consider, he ordered two suites, one for him and one for me. We started going out every night. But I always ended up going back to the hotel alone because he would always disappear with whom and to where, no one knew. My life became a trap he had set.

He wouldn't lose any occasion to call the press and alert them to our nights out, and there were always pictures of us in the paper. I tried to keep my spirit high even though we were fighting a lot. For him, any excess was acceptable. I was supposed to stay silent and simply pay the bills. Everything was proceeding according to his plan.

I was now alone, isolated, with no friends or family to turn to. I was scared for the first time in my life.

Meanwhile in my country, reports would arrive via newspapers and radio about massive demonstrations and riots, the handywork of secret agents who were being paid by a neighboring country. The intent of this regime was very clear: to invade and to annex our country to steal our wealth and natural resources and to capture their former empress, who was very popular among her people.

My family found itself in a state of danger that they had never experienced before. The sad end of other royal families close to us made my mother decide to leave the country to avoid the bloodshed of our people and organize the resistance. Our friend, the empress, was also convinced to leave by my mother.

As soon as my mother heard that the empress didn't want to leave, she went personally to visit her and said, "My dear friend, you must come with us now! You have suffered enough already. You survived a revolution, but you will not withstand the blow of another!"

The empress was convinced and joined her family in the car and left for port.

The invasion took place, and our small army could not repel it. We had never been to war before. The days before my family left were frantic. Nobody, I think, slept during the few days of the siege. To rescue resources, to organize the resistance, to rescue as many people as possible, destroy private documents—these were the priorities.

I was worried and asked to return immediately to my country to stay close to my family, but the ambassador declined my request on legal grounds. He told me that I had signed a state document and it was impossible to repeal. Alfredo also was very against this idea of me returning. He screamed at me that a return didn't make sense and that I should just wait for my family to arrive.

My mother, meanwhile, had found a little time to write to me. The telegram said:

"My son, it is with great sorrow that I announce that we are about to leave our beloved homeland. From now on, you must rely on your own strength. We are no longer in a position to maintain our agreement. Every resource left to us must be committed to liberate our country. God protects you. –Mother"

When I received the telegram, Alfredo and I were about to go out. I said nothing at the time, but I had my heart in my throat. We arrived in the ballroom, and soon I walked away from him. I could no longer endure his indifference and uncaring attitude and tried to think about what to do next. What was the right thing to do? I went upstairs and from the colonnade, and while I observed him dancing surrounded by admirers, I started to think about what had happened to us, to our friendship.

I left without letting him know. I returned to the hotel and tried to sleep, but terrible thoughts assailed my mind—doubts about us, uncertain plans to return to my country, and how to drive out the invader.

The next day at breakfast, I told Alfredo the content of the telegram. "Alfredo," I said, "we have to change our lifestyle. You know what's happening back at home right now, and we will not receive anything anymore. The money I have left will end soon. We must first look for a less expensive accommodation and find a job as soon as possible."

He didn't say anything at first, but then he told me, "Well then, we start to look for another place to live."

What actually happened was not surprising: He simply packed up, took all the money that we kept in the hotel safe, and disappeared. I never saw him again, ever.

I woke up with this shocking surprise, but I had no time to even think about it. I still had some money in the bank. With Alfredo gone, I reorganized my life. I reduced costs to a bare minimum, started to look for an apartment, and waited for the arrival of my family. At first, I thought I could live with them. When my family finally arrived in Paris, they were installed into our former embassy, which fortunately had been the personal property of my grandmother and now belonging to my mother.

· · ·

I first heard the news from a little boy who was shouting aloud the headlines of the newspaper: "Royal Family Arrives Safely." I bought a copy, and I saw a large picture of my mother entering the embassy. After seeing the front page, I wanted to see my family immediately. I set off for the embassy. When I was near, I could see the embassy looming at the end of the street. I ran towards it, but at the gate I was stopped.

The guard politely told me they had orders not to let me in. The embassy is a national territory, and I had signed to leave this territory. I could not enter unless with the permission of parliament.

I could not believe it! Given the circumstances, I thought that some rules would have made no sense, but obviously, I was wrong. I was devastated. I went back to the hotel in tears. I couldn't stop. Losing everything is one thing, but being rejected by your own family is another. I was able to see past the fence and through the windows of the ground floor. There I could see flashes of my brothers, sisters, nieces, and nephews in the windows. They didn't see me. I could not calm down to think rationally about my future. It was the first time that I had to decide on my own about what to do next. I was the architect of my own destiny; it was up to me alone. Mea culpa if I didn't make the right one.

I decided to go for a long walk, and at a certain point I saw a cinema and decided to go in to calm down. Before the movie, they showed a documentary about London, saying how big, beautiful, and full of opportunities it was. It almost looked like a sign, as if my grandmother was telling me from heaven, "Go, go to London to start your new life." So that's what I did.

"I will change my name and my clothes. I will grow my hair longer," I thought. "And I may have the chance to be happy and be loved again."

I returned to the hotel. I asked the staff to prepare the bill and to call the bank to pay. I rushed into my room to take my suitcases that were ready as I thought I would be with my family that evening. Downstairs the doorman told me with great sadness that unfortunately there was not enough money in the bank to pay the bill. I was free to go, but they would keep all the bags until I was able to pay them. People who till the day before were extremely polite because I had money, today showed coldness and delight in seeing my change in circumstances. I kept myself together and found all the courage possible. I thanked the manager and walked away towards the railway station. It was pouring rain as often happens in Paris. I felt strangely happy. After all, I no longer needed my clothes and uniforms. They represented my past. I needed new clothes for my new life in a new setting. I decided to die and to be reborn with a new name. I could change everything.

Just a few minutes before getting out of my hotel room, the receptionist passed me a call. It was Claudia. It is true that the Lord shows his divine providence when you least expect it. We always remained in touch despite my sudden departure and her disappointment. She informed me that she was married now and she was planning to have a baby soon. I was genuinely happy for her, and I wished all the best. We discussed my situation and my plan to move to London.

She gave me then the address of a lady who rented rooms. "You will be fine there," she said, "and she is not expensive and her house is near a beautiful park."

"Thank you, Claudia. I will give you news as soon as I am settled."

I reached la Gard du Nord. When the train began moving and the first people on the platform slid away, followed by the city, my nerves gave way. For some time, I could not stop my tears. I was painfully sorry for everything, for the past, for myself. I could not imagine what the future would be. When I arrived at Victoria Station in London, no one was there to meet me. The royal rooms I usually passed through were closed. There was no car, and there were no footmen wearing their livery waiting for me. It was the beginning of my new life. This time for real.

• • •

The address Claudia had given me was large and must have been very nice once. The years had caught up with it, and it needed serious restorations. With all the help gone, it can be said that the house was no longer its former, cleaner self. To add to this disheveled site, there were about ten cats inside and even more living outside of it. Some had names. Others could sleep with her in her bed, and others came into the house to eat.

The owner, Mrs. Natasha, opened the door. She was a very eccentric painter from Russia. She was short in stature, plump, with tiny little hands and feet. She moved in a comical way, like she was waltzing. She wore clothes certainly from her youth that she had re-worked which gave them a patchwork appearance. Her matted hair was pulled up and held together by a comb of diamonds, which she wore all the time. The diamond comb was one of her few remaining possessions from a past that was never coming back. It was a sort of anchor, if you will, but for memories only.

Every morning, right before breakfast, she came out in her dressing gown to get milk. In London at that time, it was still delivered outside the door in those classic, beautiful, transparent glass bottles.

You see, Natasha's family had lived in Africa until she was 20. After the death of her father, she had returned to England with her mother and younger sister. When she was left alone, she began to rent rooms because, although of a great and recognized talent, she did not want to sell her paintings.

She did not know who I was, but she knew who had given me the address. She could tell where I was from because of my accent, and she proceeded to mock me for it. I also think she enjoyed watching me eating her disgusting soup made with leftovers that I ate out of politeness. Actually, Natasha had no empty rooms to rent when I arrived. She told me that I could have the attic she used as a storeroom, and breakfast and dinner were included. I decided to take it. We left the living room where she received me, a large room with an adjoined conservatory overlooking the small park behind, and we went upstairs to see my room. The house, on three floors, seemed, with its rather narrow staircase, more like a small castle than a Victorian house.

Her first impression of the room was that it seemed very romantic. The bed was in the left corner just below a window; I thought about seeing falling stars as I feel asleep. There was also a small Victorian fireplace that gave me a hard time before I could make it work. There was no closet, only boxes everywhere, trunks and clothes from different eras. There were also theater costumes and old, wooden stage sets. Natasha was once a stage and costume designer for theaters and opera houses.

I dropped my suitcases, took a bath, and went to bed. The framework and the mattress were so old that I had to put the mattress on the floor. The springs of the mattress kept poking me, so I slept on only one side of the bed. The next day, breakfast was served in the dining room, a smaller space that overlooked the main entrance of the house. Natasha's silver cutlery was so black you could barely recognize it. Each plate used to belong to a different entire set. She used to tell us stories about what had happened, who had given them, and much more. One dish-set was given to her family by some African or Indian royalty; others were bought in some luxury department stores around the world.

I thought these were fascinating stories and true anyway. No one could deny she'd had an adventurous life that was full of surprises. I greeted the guests and the hostess and went to explore the neighborhood. The center of the area I was now living in was small but had everything you could wish for: a church, a bakery, a bank, a post office, a few small cafes, a French restaurant, and a cinema.

The nicest thing, as Claudia told me, was the park. It was big, full of trees, a small pond, and squirrels that approached you if you'd offer them food. There was also a small café attached to the bridge you had to take if you wanted to go on the other side of the park. I soon became friend with the owner. Ray was his name. He was only a few years older than me. He was a handsome guy with black hair, and he was very kind and generous. His four staff members were chosen more to fit his own bohemian way of seeing life. I went there to eat lunch almost every day, and later, only for Sunday brunch. The very relaxed family atmosphere, the good, simple food, and the kindness of the staff made this café a little oasis of warmth.

The days passed, and the financial resources were gradually thinning. Almost every week I wrote from the café a letter to my mother hoping for a change of luck. In my heart, I was still hoping to return home.

Of all the things I had now to learn to do by myself, the one I remember with particular emotion was the laundromat. Every Sunday I used to go with my big bag of dirty clothes in a laundromat on my way to Ray's. After setting the machines, I would brunch at Ray's café until they were finished. The manager of this laundromat, a rare modernity in those days, was a lady in her fifties who was very poorly dressed. She seemed neglected both in appearance and spirit. My roommates had warned me: "She never smiles and does not speak with anyone." It was true! But there was something in her eyes and in the rude way she responded to people that did not convince me. I didn't give up and decided to enquire into her quiet, lonely heart.

I decided to give her something to relax. It was clear to me that she had nothing but the laundry to manage. I didn't even know if she actually had a home or if she was sleeping in the back of the shop.

Every time I went there, I carried with me a magazine that I would pretend to forget so she could have something to read and relax. After a few weeks, she was still silent, but I noticed something between us had changed. When I returned from brunch to move laundry from the washing machine into the dryer, I saw it was already dried, folded, and ready to be taken away.

I was moved, and I looked at the lady and said, "Thank you!"

She looked at me, turned back, and without saying a word walked back into the room behind the shop where she was living. It didn't really matter that she didn't speak to me. The important thing was that I was able to get her to acknowledge me. It made my day!

I decided to move further. I wanted to give a gift, a gift to make her feel better. After a couple of weeks, I went back to do my laundry, and

I started to talk to her. I said, "Excuse me Madame, the hairdresser at the end of the road gave me this free voucher, but it's for ladies so I can't use it. Would you mind taking it for me?" I wasn't sure if she would accept or be completely mad with me.

She said nothing, and didn't move. Then I decided to leave the present on the bench and said that if she didn't want it, she could give to someone else. Then I left.

I decided to plot with the hairdresser and organize a voucher so she could have her hair done for free. I must say, with all sincerity, that the first time I saw her, the thing that looked worst about her was her hair. She had cut it badly by herself, and it was colored a tremendous yellow. She was wearing secondhand clothes and broken shoes, but I could see that behind that mask there was a beautiful face and a beautiful soul. I was determined to show her love, to show that someone cared about her, that she wasn't alone.

The following Sunday was my triumph. She appeared with her hair done and wearing a dress instead of the laundry uniform. She looked at me like she never had and smiled as she returned to her room. For the first time, I saw a smile in her face. It lighted the room and warmed my heart. I was happy. Being able to make her smile was enough for me for now. We continued to smile at each other in silence till Christmas Eve. I took the courage to stop her and ask her a few questions. I don't know if it was the Christmas spirit or the idea that both of us would have been alone on Christmas day, but I was determined to exchange at least a few words.

"Madame," I said, "I have a Christmas card for you."

She took it, smiled at me, and started to read it aloud. It was the first time I heard her voice. The card said: "Dear Madam, thanks for taking care of my laundry the past few weeks. You have been nothing but kind and gentle to me. Merry Christmas. –Leopold."

She burst into tears and started to talk. "Thank you and excuse me if I have not talked to you before. I haven't even thanked you for the hair. But you see, since I was only 15 years old I have lived in this country without family, and since I didn't speak the language well, I protected myself by not talking to anyone. People laughed at me for my accent, and despite all my effort to learn the language, people reminded me that I wasn't from here. That was England when I arrived, my dear, and I am afraid to say very little has changed."

I decided to invite her for tea, and she accepted.

We sat down at Ray's café. She was really embarrassed at first. The usual clientele was perhaps a bit too chic for her taste, but I took her arm and she felt better. I could see she was ready to tell me her story, her life. I told her I spoke her native language to give her more confidence and also to give us more privacy.

• • •

"I was born on a Mediterranean island where women have no rights but many obligations. When I was 15, I fell in love with a boy, I didn't understand the consequences. I was very naïve, so he teased me, used me, and left me. I could not understand why in loving him I was ruined, and he could not marry, even if it was him insisting all the time. It is something that still doesn't make any sense to me—the absurdity of a backward-minded society. When I discovered I was pregnant, my mother made me leave for England trusting a family where I could work as maid and take care of my baby at the same time. Unfortunately, the reality was quite different.

"Before I left, my Mother said to me: 'From now on, you are death to us, to me and to everyone else, so never come back.' When I arrived in London, there was no family waiting for me. Desperate, I turned to a pastor in the nearest church for help. He was very kind and arranged a place for me in an institute where I could stay till I had my baby. He also helped me to find the job at the launderette.

"The child was taken away from me. Social services gave it up for adoption because they said I was too young to raise him and I didn't have enough to support both of us. I was working so hard, trying to save every year to get my baby back. When I thought I had enough to raise my son, they said I could not have him back because he was well settled. Something in me died that day—the will to fight, the desire for emancipation, the desire to get my son back. During all these years, I learned to forgive my mother because I read so many stories of other girls from my country, killed by their fathers, brothers, and uncles. I understood the gesture of my mother. My mother loved me. My mother was modern and decided to save my life because she loved me".

We carried on chatting for a while, finished our tea with the lovely homemade cake, and said goodbye. We held hands for few moments and left.

In Natasha's attic that night, I couldn't sleep. Looking at the stars and the gigantic moon, thinking about how excited I was about the conversation I'd had with the laundry lady. I kept thinking about her son, her story. I wanted to do something, but what? What I could possibly do without creating chaos in their lives? That same evening, I called Claudia, the only close friend I had left, and from whom I could ask for an impartial view. I picked up the phone that was on top of a large Louis Vuitton trunk at the entrance of the house. I dialed the number and luckily, she answered. Claudia's advice was, as always, perfect.

She said, "Track down first her son. See his current situation, how he has been and how he is now. Only then, judge if it is appropriate to introduce them."

And so I did.

It was not very difficult to trace the boy because Claudia had given me plenty of tips to track him down. I discovered he was working in a shoes, gloves, and hats store, one of those very traditional gentleman's stores London once had plenty of. I went there with the excuse of buying a new pair of shoes, and I started to ask some questions, pretending I was a talkative customer. His name was Joe, and he was very gentle and seemed to enjoy our small talk while I was trying on shoes. He noticed my ring and said he liked it a lot, and I spotted an opportunity for deeper investigations.

I made up a story on the spot and replied, "This is from my mother, but it was given to me when I was put in an orphanage. I would do anything to meet her, if she is still alive."

"What a coincidence," he replied, "my story is very similar, but I was adopted right after my birth and never met my real mother. I would give everything to meet her."

"That so sweet. I hope, one day, we both have the chance to hug them."

"I hope so too," he concluded.

I paid for the shoes and left. I found out later he had inherited the shop from his adopted parents that had both passed away. He also lived on the other side of the park with his wife and three children.

The day after, I gathered my courage and went to see the lady. I offered tea at Ray's again. I cautiously started to talk. "Madame, I have some good news. I managed to track down your son. I know where he lives, where he works, and if you want, we can go and see him."

The lady, tearfully and with a disarming purity of the heart, answered, "But I can't go out like this."

So tender was her reply, it reminded me of when Cinderella says to her Fairy Godmother that she can't go to the ball without a dress. She continued, "I would like to see him, but I am scared. Do you think we can visit him at the shop?"

"Yes," I replied, "of course we can. He works in a shop not too far from here. We will go there to look for a pair of gloves."

The morning after, I paid someone to take her shift, and we spent all day to buying new clothes, shoes, gloves, and a hat. Then we went to a beauty salon where they took care of her hair, hands, and makeup. When they finished, she looked twenty years younger, as if they had cancelled out all the suffering in her life.

Now ready, we took a cab and went to her son's shop. When we were there, the lady froze for a moment. She stopped outside the entrance, perhaps having second thoughts. While she was trying to look inside through the window, to see if she could spot him first, she whispered, "No, no, let's not enter. What if I disturb his peace?"

"You are giving him peace at last. He wants to meet you, and always wondered where you were. It is something he has waited for all his life and will give him peace and happiness. It is your time to have happiness too."

I entered the store first and said a few words with Joe who recognized me from the previous visit. The lady came in behind me, looked at her son, and fainted.

She had seen the resemblance to her own father when he was young, how she remembered him when she left. Gently, Joe helped her to sit down in a green velvet chaise longue and ran for some fresh water. When he came back, the lady had already opened her eyes. They looked at each other in inexplicable silence.

Then I felt it was time to intervene. "My dear Joe," I said, "you told me that your adoptive parents have been very good to you and that they passed away not too long ago. Well, now it is your time to meet the person who gave your life." With a slight movement of the hand I pointed the lady.

My words and tone may have been a bit theatrical, but it worked. The man's eyes widened, and he said "Mummy?" He fell to the ground and hugged her knees.

What happened after I don't know because I wanted to leave them alone. I would return another time.

We all met again a few days later in Joe's house. By then, she had moved into her son's home and stopped working at the launderette. It was finally her time to rest.

Meanwhile, my situation wasn't improving at all. I was cut out completely. From time to time, I read in the newspapers or magazines articles about my family, but I was never mentioned. It seemed like I had never existed, erased from the tree forever. I went to the bank, and I realized I had very little money left, enough for a month or two. I stopped hoping I could return home and started looking for a job, but luck wasn't on my side. I spent nearly two months looking for a job and went on thousands of job interviews without any success. One day I was walking, not knowing what to do and where to go, when I saw on a bench a newspaper someone left there with a picture of my beloved Aunt Giovanna on the cover. She had passed away.

I grabbed it and started to read. I was happy to see she passed away in her bed without pain. I know it sounds crazy, but I looked at the sky and saw her, a gigantic, cloudy image smiling at me! I prayed to her to help me, and after I carried on reading the newspaper, I saw an advertisement for a Christmas sales position. It was only for a month, but it was better than nothing. It was in the same department store where I had bought clothes for the lady of the launderette. Miraculously, I got the job. The department store had six floors with all sorts of merchandise. I was assigned to the ground floor to sell men clothes. My good nature, good manners, and good education helped me take steps forward career-wise. First, my Christmas job was extended into a full-time position. Later on, I was promoted to manager of an in-shop boutique.

My life started to have a quiet routine: wake up very early, get ready, coffee and croissant in the local bakery next to the church, metro to work, lunch break at noon, returning home at 8:00 P.M., dinner with Natasha and the rest of the lodgers, and finally to bed. I had a life and a job, and I could finally not worry about being homeless as this was my worst recurrent nightmare.

The last two months had been very hard indeed. I'd had hardly any money except to pay the rent, and some days I went downtown for some job interviews without a penny in my pockets. I'd had to walk, and since we were quite far from the center, I was walking for four or five hours before reaching my destination. My meals were those provided by Natasha, and I was walking around and skipping lunch. My daily pocket search for coins in trousers or jackets gave me enough for a coffee or some water.

The department store where I was working had a cafeteria on the top floor with a beautiful terrace and an even more beautiful view of London. I had lunch there every day at noon. One day, I noticed seated in front of me a very elegant and distinct-looking younger man intently reading a book. He seemed familiar. But then I thought that would be impossible considering the place where we both were. I tried to get his attention. I wanted to know him. But he kept his eyes on his book. I discovered later when we became friends that he was simply an avid reader. I began to sit next to him every day, trying to discover in which floor and department he was working. It wasn't easy. He always stayed longer than me in the cafeteria, reading. Once I saw him in the smoking room chatting with a friend as I passed by and stared at him. He noticed it. I couldn't stop admiring his gentle and graceful manners, his beautiful blue eyes, and his ginger hair. This was when he noticed me for the first time. I thought now he wouldn't be my friend, that must have thought I was weird.

In the back of each floor, there was a stock room where the merchandise was stored, as well as items they put on hold. One day, a lucky one, a very rich and equally rude lady came into my boutique. After purchasing shirts for her husband, she asked me to go and get tablecloths she purchased on the second floor. She said she would wait for me. Being the manager, I said yes and went up to the second floor. I asked my colleague where the shopping bags were, and he said they were in the stockroom. I went inside.

While I was still looking, I heard a thud. I walked over to the sound and saw a mountain of towels fall on another colleague there perhaps for a similar or same reason. I got closer to him and gave my hand to help him to get up and found myself face-to-face with the young man. His wonderful eyes, sweet smile, and his embarrassment warmed my heart. In taking his hand, I noticed he was wearing a ring with a coat of arms. I couldn't believe my eyes. I knew that crest. It was a famous one. I knew who it belonged to and what had happened to that family.

I called a colleague. I asked her the favor of delivering the bags to my client, to apologize for me, and to tell her I had been detained by a little accident. Meanwhile, I said to the manager of the second floor that it was my fault that the towels had fallen. I decided to stay with him to help with the mess, and I noticed he had a slight problem walking. Something was wrong with one of his feet.

I thought, *"No, he can't be."*

The person the ring used to belong to was a classic ballet dancer that I saw so many times at the opera. It could be a coincidence, or perhaps he was his brother. I remember he had two, one a former office in the Russian Imperial Guard and another a musician. While having all these thoughts in my head, I continued helping him put everything in order.

When we finished, I took courage and I invited him for a beer after work. To my delight, he agreed. We went to a pub close to work, built in an underpass in a side street. It was a typical Victorian English pub. We started talking in front of a beer and did not stop even at the stroke of midnight. We could hear in the background the lyrics of a Jimmy Walsh song:

Showing no emotion, my feelings locked inside
I made myself an island, trying to take my heart and hide
I built a wall around me, afraid of letting go
But suddenly an open door I never saw before
In your eyes
I see the light leading me home again
It's heaven in your arms, my love
My heart is in your hands
In your eyes
Seems so right, I see forever in your smile
This man is a child again (In your eyes)

The church clock nearby reminded us that we had missed the last tram to go back home. I asked him to spend the night at my place, since he lived so far away.

"You must accept, please. Otherwise you will not have enough sleep," I said.

We took a cab to Natasha's place, and we fell asleep on the way. We arrived home and tried to stay quiet as we climbed the stairs up to my room. Instead of sleeping, we talked more while the light of the stars lit up the room. My single bed was made with two old mattresses. I put them on the floor next to each other, and we lay down. David was his name, and he told me he was the famous dancer I thought he was. Dave also told me the story of his family, what had happened to his Mom and to his two brothers during the revolution in his country, and how he had injured his foot.

Dave, as I soon started to call him, belonged to an aristocratic family as old as the emperors themselves. His father, an officer, was killed in the war when he was little, and his mother raised him and his two brothers alone. One brother followed his father's footsteps, starting a military career. Dave and his other brother followed their artistic passions encouraged by their mother—ballet for Dave and music for the other.

"The first day of the revolution," recalled Dave, "I was in the opera house studio, practicing as usual. A friend, sent by my older brother, told me to run home and stay with my mother. That was the day when rebels started to attack private homes, taking away everything they could carry and killing anyone who tried to oppose them. My heart seized up. I got on my horse at home. At first the streets were still deserted, but then I started to see crowds. I made several detours to avoid being stopped by the insurgents. I heard shots and explosions, and bullets whizzed above my head. For the first time in my life, I experienced mortal fear. I couldn't communicate with my brother, as much as I would have loved to, because he was in command of the guards on patrol at the Imperial Palace. I arrived at home, and when I opened the entrance door, I saw the staff frightened and waiting to defend themselves and the house from an attack. I climbed the staircase and went straight into my mother's room.

"Her room overlooked the inner porch of Corinthian columns that decorated the whole first floor. I found my mum seated in a chaise long reading an ancient book on Greek mythology. Our little dog, Bell, was at her feet giving her good company. She had the habit to read the news daily, so she was not completely unaware of what was going on in the country and in our city.

"When I told her what I had seen on my way home and that the situation was plummeting and we had to find a safe place to move, she replied, 'Then there is no time left. I cannot leave the house. I am still waiting for your brothers to come back home, and your father is buried here. I will depart with them. You go ahead, please. Even if we lose everything, they will not kill an old lady, and in one way or another I will reach you as soon as your brothers are here.'

"She pulled an envelope from under the pillow against which she was leaning, and she said, 'Take this money and these pearls,' she removed them from her neck, 'and my jewelry box that is on that drawer. Take your horse to Lake Nazik. Now it is frozen. When you arrive, wait for the night and then leave your horse free and continue on foot.'

"Then, she went close to her bed, took a white, big, flat fur used as a bedspread, and continued, 'Cover yourself while walking on the lake. We don't know if there are revolutionaries or loyalist at the border. Please, my son, do exactly what I told you. When you have reached the border and you will be safe and sound, take a train and go to Paris and wait for me at this address of my friend Chantal. Your brothers and I will reach you as soon as possible. Don't worry about me! They can take everything, even our home, but they are not going to kill an old lady.'

"I ran to my room to get warmer clothes, and I said goodbye to my mum and the staff. I left from the back door of the garden.

"When I arrived at the lake, it was dark. I released the horse and began to walk towards the other side of the lake as my mum had told me. A few times the security lights lit up the lake, and I threw myself down on the ground and covered myself with the big white fur that had been on my mother's bed.

"I was walking and was very tired, hungry, and sleepy. The ice broke, and my left foot fell into the icy water, causing a fracture. Despite my internal turmoil, I didn't lose it and tried instead to dry my broken foot. I put it in a splint, changed my socks, and continued to walk. I threw the wet sock into the lake. I saw the sock going down the hole, and I thought about everyone else who would have traveled this way to safety. Tears rolled down in my eyes in silence.

"I arrived in Finland and took refuge in a hotel where I was visited by a doctor who diagnosed my broken foot. Fortunately, there was no need for an amputation, but it was clear I could not dance anymore. I sank into a deep depression. In just a few days, I had lost my family, my home, and my career. To move on and overcome sadness, I kept repeating to myself, 'You are not a dancer anymore.' Despite this, I had something bigger to worry about: the fate of my family. When I recovered completely, I had to be brave and courageous to follow my mother's advice. The doctor gave me a very nice walking stick, and I took the train for Paris where I hoped to receive news of my family. When there, more devastating news was shouted in the streets of Paris by the news-standers. I read that the emperor and his family had been murdered and that everything was lost. My only thought now was to reach the house of my mother's friend and hope that they would come. I decided to start to look positively at my situation. I thought, 'We were alive, and we will manage in one way or another to overcome these sad circumstances.' I promised to myself to not speak or remember the past. While I considered my life, I started thinking what kind of job I could do to support my mother when she arrived.

"Unfortunately, the arrival in Paris didn't result in anything good as I expected. My mother's friend didn't live in her palace anymore.

The old caretaker, who remembered me and my mum very well, told me that the lady, now in poor health conditions, had been moved close to her sons in Switzerland in a nursing home and that the house had been sold to a bank, except for the concierge little cottage at the entrance of the villa that was donated to her.

"I decided then to look for a hotel. I still had the money my mum had given me at the time of separation. Short after, I found a room and went out looking for news. I sat down in a café. The latest events left me in shock: the imperial family killed, the buildings looted, and the civilians killed during the riots. Among the list of people killed, I saw my mother and one of my brothers. I still didn't believe it. After a while, one of our surviving staff told me how he managed to escape and about the last hours of my mother's life.

"The young boy said, 'Shortly after your departure, the rebels reached the entrance of the house, and after several blows they knocked it down. Your mother decided to wait for them on the first floor right on the first step of the staircase that led down to the main entrance. With each rumble of the riots, the frightened staff left the entrance and went upstairs to stay close to your mother to protect her. She was still straight and apparently motionless on the stairs. When they knocked down the door, a huge crowd poured inside and some began to shoot widely towards the stairs where we were all waiting. Your mother, in an act of compassion and with the hope to save my life, asked me to go and get a shawl to keep her warm just in case they were imprisoned. The shawl of a specific color and with specific motives in reality didn't exist. Your mother wanted to give me time to look so if events turned ugly, I could hide myself. They killed your mother first. She slumped to the ground, holding a crucifix in her hand. The hand opened almost to show it to those present. After the first gunshot, I heard many more mixed with screams for mercy. I decided to hide behind a wooden panel, and I stayed there for two days till the rebels left, taking with them anything they could. When I finally left my hiding place, I could not believe what

I saw: devastation and innocent victims lying where I had left them. I had some water and took any food I could find. Your brother, Sebastian, likely wasn't at home when the mob came. He was on duty with his soldiers who were faithful to the emperor. When he could finally leave his post, he came home. Petrified, he saw your mom and all the people of the house around her. He picked up the crucifix and put it around his neck. With the help of his soldiers, he buried everyone in the garden.

"'I saw them, and I started to scream *Sebastian, Sebastian.* When he saw me, we hugged each other, and he kissed me all over my face with joy. After we recounted each other's last days since he left, we prayed in the garden for the victims. There was no time for a mass.

"'The soldiers closed the grave with a marble cover and then left the small chapel. These were your brother's last words to me: *Take this money and leave the country as soon as possible. We can't protect you anymore. We are leaving too, God knows where.* We kissed each other, and we went separate ways.

"'I didn't see in the newspaper that my other brother's name on the list of the killed in action. I decided to move to London because I thought this is where my brother would go. He knows the language and perhaps he could hope for a position in the British Army. London replaced Paris in my plans.'"

The attraction I felt for David soon turned into friendship, and then affection. Every evening, after work, we went for a beer in what would become "our" pub. We were unstoppable. We talked for hours and hours about our lives, our past, our fears, our weaknesses, our greatest passions, and our dreams for the future. We soon discovered we had a lot of things in common, but most of all, we had an identical sensibility, the same ability to appreciate and respond to emotional and aesthetic influences. Among a number of interests, we shared the love for classical mythology, something Dave had shared and cultivated with his mom.

One evening, while walking in SoHo Square back from the pub, a gypsy with a harmonica was playing "La Vie en Rose." We looked at each other and simultaneously said, "I love this song." I don't know if it was the warm spring temperature, the street lights, the trees, the moon, or the sculpture of Charles the First, but everything felt magical. I took his hand, and we started to dance softly, and then when the song ended, we stopped.

I kissed him on the cheek, and I said: "Come and live with me."

With an immense light in his sweet blue eyes and a few tears of joy, he accepted. That same weekend, putting everything in a black cab, I helped him to move his possessions into Natasha's attic. From that moment, "La Vie en Rose" became our song.

During the trip, we were laughing and talking with a serene joy that we had both missed, a lightheartedness after terrible storms. That was for me the beginning of my truly happy life.

Neither of us had many things. After a few months, we started planning our first holiday. We were both fans of Lord Byron, so we decided on Greece. We went first to Athens. It was Dave's first time, and I was delighted to see his joy in telling me stories and identifying the heroes and philosophers. He was running from one place to another, explaining as much as possible. I was touched, for example, by his emotion in telling me, "This is where Pericles delivered his famous Funeral Oration to the Athenians after the first year of the Peloponnesian war: '*We throw open our city to the world, and never by alien acts exclude foreigners from any opportunity of learning or observing, although the eyes of an enemy may occasionally profit by our liberality.*'"

He recited it from memory.

We stayed there few minutes in respectful silence to honor ancient Athens.

After we moved to Crete. I went through a lot to convince Dave to put on a swimsuit and get into the blue sea with me. He didn't want to show his foot. It the end, I looked intensely into his eyes and asked him, "Do you trust me?"

"I do," he replied.

We jumped into the water. We spent the rest of the week waking up early in the morning, and after having breakfast at the hotel, we were at the beach till eleven o'clock before it became hot and crowded. We spent the afternoons on the edge of the hotel's pool that was almost deserted during the day. This way we avoided sunburns and prying eyes.

In the evenings, we used to go to eat in a typical Greek tavern with trees in the courtyard where the tables were located. The wooden door of the restaurant were almost in the middle of a narrow road with steps facing the main boulevard. We became regulars, and the staff soon learned our favorites and knew our orders. The owner of the restaurant always offered to us at the end of each meal the famous Greek liquor, ouzo.

After the Greek Holiday, we returned to London. Once in the house we took the mail and went into our room. Natasha, luckily, wasn't there. She was in Portugal where she was spending the summer with her sister. Dave opened a letter from the Polish police, and he burst into tears of joy. His brother, Sebastian, was alive in a hospital in Warsaw, and he needed him.

After almost a year living together and becoming everything to me, Dave and I had to part.

I told him, "Go, I am here waiting for you till your brother gets better. Then come back to me, bring your brother, and we will look for a bigger place where we can live all together."

Dave spent six months in Warsaw helping his brother to recover. I doubled the shifts at work and started to work on Sundays so I could help him while he was helping his brother. After six months, Sebastian recovered and got a job in the Polish army and decided to stay. Finally, Dave was able to return to London. The two brothers said goodbye and promised to meet again soon. Sebastian would visit us in England.

Dave's return was wonderful. I went to pick him up at the station. I rented a car, and we took off to Brighton to spend the weekend there. Crossing the English countryside was very romantic. We stopped to pray in a small church with an adjoining cemetery. We had breakfast in a Tudor-style inn with home-cooked food, seated near a large fireplace next to a patio door where we were able to glimpse the beautiful lavender garden.

We arrived in Brighton and took a room overlooking the ocean. We visited the Royal Pavilion and walked along the center of the city and the beach. As we were walking, Dave saw a line of stalls, and we decided to have a look. The stalls were mainly selling antiques and books. And Dave remarked, "If we are lucky, we may find books that are not in print anymore!"

Astonished, we found out that the stalls were managed by refugees from Dave's country, selling items brought with them. We identified items looted from friends' houses and even some from his own home. Each single small stall was for Dave, and therefore also for me, very emotional. We spent most of the rest of the afternoon there. Dave was going through each and every single book or object, trying to recall where they came from.

Suddenly, he stopped, holding a book and staring at it. He waited, and then he opened the cover and recognized the signature of his mother and the *ex libris* stamp that she used to put in each single book of her personal library. That book was the one his mum was reading the last time they had seen each other. I took it, and without saying a word, I went to the sales assistant and paid the 25 pounds, and we left.

It was time for dinner, and I decided that the book discovery was to be celebrated, not grieved. I felt the discovery of the book was a way for his mother to tell him she was always by his side. I took Dave to a nice *fin de siècle* restaurant decorated with chintz sofas and a profusion of palm trees that I hoped would make him feel at home.

The evening was a success. We had fun. We talked, ate, drank, and told anecdotes of our past lives. It was an evening to celebrate our love, the love of two people who were perfect for one another, but also of those that were gone but would stay forever in our hearts.

While I was telling my story to the student, we decided to take a break and sit in a café not too far from the university where I teach, to continue my story over a cup of tea.

"So, where was I?"

"To your weekend in Brighton, Professor," replied my student.

"Are you sure you want me to continue?"

"Yes, sir."

Well, after that wonderful weekend, we drove back home. Living with Natasha in the meantime became unbearable. At that time, I was trying to avoid her, waking up before her and coming back when she was already in bed. She thought it was fun to mock me and Dave. I was frustrated because she was old and I couldn't bring myself to correct her. Instead, I tried to avoid conflicts. My politeness only made her meaner. I was complaining to Dave all the time. "Did you see what she did to me? Did you hear what she said?"

It became too much. With his usual calm, Dave said, "Now it is time for us to find a place on our own. Natasha is really aggravating. I understand how she gets on your nerves. She is always nice to me because she knows me and probably she came to see me dancing. Being a costume designer, I am sure she saw me dancing before the revolution. Tomorrow we will look for an apartment just for us."

Our finances were still very limited, so we had to settle for a house a colleague told us about. We thought he was the owner, but we were wrong. We found out later that he was illegally using the property. At that time, the mayor was giving flats to those who would take care of orphan children, but instead of giving to the children, he was using that house for his own profit and keeping them all in his own house.

One night, we were awakened by a telephone call. It was our colleague telling us to leave the house immediately because the police were investigating him.

"Police? Why police?"

"The flat is not mine," he said and hung up.

In a bit of panic, we discussed what to do, and Dave had the best idea.

"There is no need to go on the street now. The inspectors will certainly not come at 2:00 A.M. but tomorrow morning. Let's do it this way. We go back to sleep, get up early, and prepare our bags. When we go to work, we will leave them in the warehouse of the department store."

That morning, we woke up at 5:00 A.M., prepared our luggage, put everything into two taxis, and headed to work. I talked to the warden. I explained the situation, and very kindly he said to me that he could keep our belongings for the day. In the evening, we had to take them with us.

During the day, we began to ask our colleagues if they had space in their garages and some offered to help. That night, again in two taxis, we visited five colleagues and dropped off some things. That same day, we discovered we were not the only ones scammed by that man. We left the taxi near the British Museum, and we started looking for a hotel for the night. The money left in our pockets after paying taxis was very little. We ended up in a hostel with a shared bathroom, but at least we had a room just for both of us. It was the only thing we could afford at the time.

A few days after, we read about the, so-called by the press, "Scandal of the ...."

Our "landlord" didn't work. He was living with government money by adopting abandoned children or children with disabilities.

That same Sunday, we went to eat at Ray's in Greenwich. We needed a break and we wanted to walk in the park.

While having brunch, Ray talked to us, and we told him about the trouble. He said, "I read about the scandal and the trafficking of children, but I could not ever imagine that you were living in one of his scammed flats. Luckily, both your names, as tenants, have not come out."

I replied, "We left the house at 6:00 A.M. and found out that the police arrived at 10:00."

Ray, a friend, offered us a place to stay. "Guys, listen, I have a guest room, and I am always here at the café and you at your work. It will be easy." It felt like a godsend. We moved that night, and the following Sunday we recovered our personal belongings scattered in the garage of our colleagues. We were now safe in a friend's house.

Five or six serene years passed by. We spent our days off in museums, cinemas, theatres, opera houses, and bookstores and travelling when we could. Paydays we went shopping, not in the stores where we used to, but in new ones more suitable for our budget.

"Have you heard enough, dear?" I asked to my student.

"Not entirely, Professor," he replied. "When did you started teaching, and why did you move to this country?"

"I really have to go," I said, smiling, "But first let me have another cup of tea. Do you want another too? Two more please, you are really very curious."

"It is so fascinating for me," said the student, "that no one knows who either of you are."

"Luckily," I replied. "People forget too easily. Who knows nowadays what the last Grand Duke of Tuscany looked like or the last King of Two Sicilies? Anonymity has allowed many of us to start a new life, and so it is for David and I."

Now that we had a house, or at least a room shared with friends, we had to think about what to do next, our future, and work on stability. We discussed and looked into our personal talents, characteristics, and passions. I know it may sounds strange to you, but at the end, after a long analysis and evaluating different alternatives, we both concluded that we had qualities, knowledge, studies, and experiences to become excellent teachers. Dave's degrees in speech and drama helped him to find a teaching job in an academy for actors while I started teaching history of art at a university.

Our last day at work in the department store was very moving. We knew lots of people and it took all day to say goodbye to everyone. We were well-liked, and they saw the love that united us and how well we took care of each other. We received farewell gifts, greeting cards, and even some envelopes with money. We were both delighted, and Dave and I soon made new friends in new workplaces, but we didn't change our habits or routines very much.

Every morning, Dave made coffee and brought it to me in bed, because I always found it very hard to wake up in the morning. This one of many simple gestures of affection helped me to regain serenity. I remember one morning he gave me the best gift of my life. He left for his academy, and he called me at work from a booth that was near the bus stop.

He said quickly, "In ten minutes, walk out of the university front door and watch the bus as it passes." He was very cheerful.

"Okay, okay", I said smiling. "In 10 minutes, I will be outside the main entrance."

When the bus passed by, I saw him over in the window greeting me with one hand and holding with the other against the glass window of the bus a paper on which he'd written, "I Love You." He was smiling, completely happy, and serene. We had taken the right path. I could not hold tears. It was the sweetest thing anyone ever done for me.

Two years late, we organized a European tour by car. Our idea was to trace Lord Byron's footsteps from England to Greece. Dave and I studied Ancient Greece, but we were eager to learn about the modern one. The car was an unexpected legacy of my grandmother that was sent to me from Paris. We enrolled in a course taught by a professor from the University of Athens in a monastery over the summer.

We soon become friends, and we felt we could confide in him. He took our curriculum vitae and promised us that once he was back at home, he would talk to his boss and see if we could teach in Athens. A few weeks later, we returned to London and forgot all about it.

A quiet Friday in October, I went to collect the mail from the box while Dave was preparing breakfast. There was a letter from the University of Athens that I recognized first from the beautiful stamp of King Paul of Greece. We were both overjoyed. We had a job in our spiritual home: Greece.

"What time is it my dear?"

"It is 7:00 P.M., Professor".

"Oh my God, it is very late. I have to go now".

"Professor, please promise me we will continue this conversation. There are so many things I want to ask you".

"Okay, dear, but now I have to go".

The professor greeted his pupil and walked through the department corridor where Dave was still teaching. Soon after, he too finished and walked out of his class. They looked at each other eyes with the same light that had been there in the stockroom, years ago.

They smiled at each other, and Leo asked, "Shall we go home? Let me carry your bag, please."

"Thank you," Dave replied.